398·2

0575 042613 5667 DC

leprechauns, legends and irish tales

leprechauns, legends and irish tales

hugh mcgowan

illustrated by peter haigh

LONDON · VICTOR GOLLANCZ LTD · 1988

For Mary, Yvonne, Nicole and David

First published in Great Britain 1988
by Victor Gollancz Ltd
14 Henrietta Street, London WC2E 8QJ

Text © Hugh McGowan 1988
Illustrations © Peter Haigh 1988

British Library Cataloguing in Publication Data
McGowan, Hugh
    Leprechauns, legends and Irish tales.
    1. Tales—Ireland   2. Legends—Ireland
    I. Title
    398.2'09415   GRI53.5
    ISBN 0-575-04261-3

Photoset by Rowland Phototypesetting Ltd
Bury St Edmunds, Suffolk
Printed and bound in Singapore for
Imago Publishing Ltd

ACKNOWLEDGEMENTS

In the making of a book, many people contribute in small ways and help to change an ambition into reality. In particular I would like to thank the following:

firstly Mae Sullivan who suggested the project; her brother Larry Shine for his practical advice; a host of fellow teachers helped in myriad ways— Brian Farley, Ted O'Loughlin, Kevin Murtagh, Colm Baker, Shea Mullally; Margaret Murphy who diligently typed a difficult manuscript; Niall Buckley for his professional advice.

Peter Haigh wishes to extend a special word of thanks to Annie, Mel, Kevin and Ann Mary.

lepRechauns,
legends and
iRish tales

contents

introduction

The land of Ireland today lies freckled with
reminders of a very old past. Touring through the
countryside, the traveller finds cairn, tower,
monastery and castle—physical evidence of life
stretching back to prehistoric times. Touch the
weathered stone of a round tower or peep into the
gloom of a megalithic tomb and you feel a
reverence, a respect for the sheer durability of
these sturdy structures. Standing within such
ancient walls, it is difficult to restrain one's
imagination from making a leap backwards in
time, and entering an Ireland of myth and legend.

Irish folklore began over two thousand years ago
as an oral tradition. Some of the myths from which
the tales evolved are older, indeed, than the
megaliths. The oldest date back to the Early
Mythological Cycle—a time of violence and
superstition. These stories concern the Tuatha De
Danann, an heroic race of warriors who lived in
Ireland before the Celts. Their deeds were mighty
and their natures divine. But they were defeated at
the second Battle of Moytura by Fomorian
invaders led by Balor of the Evil Eye. Balor was an
evil magician who had a secret weapon, a third eye
which could blast fire when exposed. The defeated
Tuatha De Danann were banished underground by
their Fomorian overlords, only to emerge, years
later, as dwarfed men with uncanny powers. These
descendants are the Leprechauns and Fir Darrigs
of Irish Folklore.

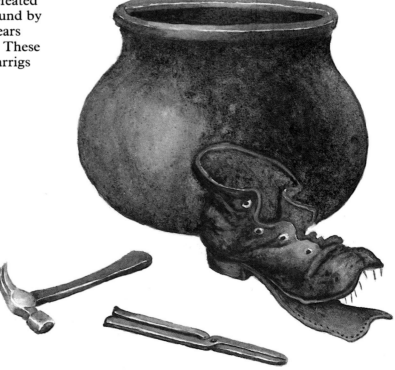

Leprechauns and Fir Darrigs are distinctive fairies, far removed from the more delicate varieties with famous addresses at the bottom of the garden. These Irish fairies have human bodies, though they stand only three feet high. Both possess a wry humour. In fact, they are almost human, until they vanish or lead you astray or afflict you with some irritating ailment.

The Leprechaun is a dour cranky cobbler who lives alone. He is old, small and dresses in green. He claims to make shoes for the Sidhe (tiny fairies who live in underground forts), but he seldom seems to complete a pair. He is famous for his hidden crock of gold, but to find this you must first catch the Leprechaun, and this is not easy for he delights in tantalising greedy people. Usually he tricks them, and disappears.

The Fir Darrig (Red Man) is similarly dwarfish, but he dresses in red. He likes to have fun. He usually lives in the space between the ceiling and thatch of cottages and he is always up to mischief. He loves a dance or a jig and enjoys a drink. He is always smiling, but sometimes you feel he may be laughing at you—not with you. He has magical powers: He may offer you three wishes. But be careful how you choose because, although he has the power to grant them, he will be watching for ways to disappoint you. However, he seems more endearing than most Leprechauns and he will do a good turn to a deserving cause.

These old stories of Irish Folklore have their base in the history of the Early Mythological Cycle. In Pre-Christian Ireland, old druidic creeds spawned many wizards and man's imagination travelled a road lined with mystery, superstition and fear. This eerie world is reflected in the characters of the Pooka and the Banshee.

Sometimes the Pooka appears in these stories, sometimes you just sense he is present—but there will never be a warning of his arrival. When he does materialise, his physique is immense and hairy, for he can take on different shapes: sometimes he's a bull, a horse, a goat, a donkey, a snake, a vague hairy back to ride on. He will whisk the unsuspecting on an uncomfortable ride through the starry night, travelling across continents at the speed of sound. In other tales the Pooka doesn't take a shape: you know he is there but you can't see or touch him. He is a rush of wind: an invisible menace. But, however he appears, the Pooka is to be avoided; he is uncontrollable and unpredictable.

The Banshee is a spirit whose sad song warns of imminent death. She takes the shape of a beautiful girl dressed in flowing white and has a siren quality which attracts the listener in spite of its sad prophecy. She appears and disappears on dark windy nights and those who hear her chant know that a death will shortly follow.

These are the characters of the ancient tales, and as the old storyteller used to say, "If there's a word of a lie in it, so be it! It was not I who invented it."

leprechauns: what are they like?

Walking down a country lane on a summer's afternoon is a very pleasant experience. The scene is a peaceful one and the silence is broken only by the chirp of crickets in the long grass and the cropping of grass as cattle graze a nearby field. But listen carefully. A tap-tap-tapping, accompanied by grumblings and mutterings. The hedge is thick but you catch a glimpse of movement beyond. You run down the road to a gap in the hedge, lean over and there he is. Sitting cross-legged, mouth full of tacks and little hammer tap-tapping away, Irish folklore's most famous citizen—the Leprechaun.

The name *Leprechaun* is Gaelic for *shoemaker* and, as the shoe he makes is tiny, he is thought to be shoemaker for the fairies. The old books of Irish folklore tell us that he is 'a tiny man, though not so small that he could hide under a mushroom or dance on a blade of grass.' Old Bridget Cleary from Galway, who has seen many a Leprechaun in her day, describes him thus: "he is a yard or so in height and small in stature for a man. I've seen children bigger, fine lumps of boys and girls who have been careful to eat their porridge every morning."

Sean McDermot, an old farmer from the Mourne mountains, recalls seeing several leprechauns at dusk one stormy evening: "They were little creatures with red hair, about the size of children."

From such testimony and that of other witnesses, we know that a leprechaun is small, but quite human in appearance. He will dress in an old-fashioned green frock coat with seven large silver buttons. His trousers come to the knee where they are met by white stockings. His footwear is curly-toed with large silver buckles. He has a three-cornered hat like a highwayman and wears a leather apron, a sign of his cobbling trade. All witnesses have been struck by his distinctive face. Sean McDermot again supplies the details: "His countenance is a mixture of crankiness and humour. He has a pair of piercing black eyes which twinkle with mirth or mischief. His nose is hooked and his mouth grins from ear to ear. I'll never forget his squeaky voice, as sharp as a thorn bush."

When the leprechaun has been spotted, he will often continue working, his mouth full of tacks, and he will quite ignore the observer. The tools of his trade will be scattered in the grass around him.

A Leprechaun carries two purses. In one there is a silver shilling—this coin magically returns to the purse every time it has been paid out, so that the Leprechaun can seem to be paying out large sums of money without ever losing his shilling. In the other purse he puts a common copper coin with which he first attempts to bribe his way out of tricky situations. If this offer is turned down, he produces the silver shilling. The unlucky recipient returns home, only to find the coin has mysteriously vanished from their pocket.

Many's the story that's been told of the leprechaun's tricks and guiles. His long life (leprechauns are reputed to live to three hundred years) is spent collecting and hoarding every penny and amassing treasure. The resulting large fortune is placed in a crock and buried. Only the leprechaun knows the crock's location, and he won't reveal this without a struggle.

Rumour has it that the crock of gold is buried at the bottom of the rainbow, but there are many rainbows in Ireland. Your only chance to find the treasure is to catch a leprechaun. The secret is to creep up on him as he whistles at his work and to grab him tightly and never take your eyes off him. He will pretend to be calm and unruffled, but all the time he is thinking madly of how he might escape. He will promise readily to tell where his treasure is buried, but be careful you don't relax your grip. Hold him tight and stare at him hard because, if you don't, he will vanish quicker than you can say, 'Bacon and Cabbage'.

A story is told of Claire McIvor, a young Kerrywoman, who was lucky enough to stumble across a leprechaun, and she returning home one warm summer's evening. She was to be married within the week and as she stood there in the field clutching the leprechaun, her mind filled with thoughts of all the fine dishes she could buy for her dresser if only this silly little leprechaun would give her his crock of gold.

"If ye don't tell me where your gold is hidden," says she, "I'll squeeze the gizzard out o' ye."

"Wait a bit, wait a bit," said the leprechaun. "Sure I'll tell ye and welcome. But a small slip of a girl like you would never carry it home for 'tis fierce heavy."

"Never mind your blarney now," said Claire. "Give over your gold and let me do the worrying of getting it home."

"Fair enough, fair enough," said the leprechaun and his gaze became locked on the crest of the hill behind her.

"Isn't that your *intended* coming over the hill? A fine big fella he is. Sure he'll transport the gold and no bother."

As Claire turned to search the skyline, the leprechaun squirmed loose. There was no *intended* in the vicinity and the leprechaun's squeaks of laughter echoed from the next field.

So greedy people who want the leprechaun's gold face a formidable foe. He is clever and slippery and can recognise immediately the hidden motives deep in men's hearts. In all the tales concerning this elusive fairy, one truth emerges—you won't get your hands on his gold without a fierce struggle.

"Stranger sight than I can tell—Oh! A little merry
  fellow,
With nose and cheeks most mellow, is seated all
  alone
O'er a broken shoe low bending, mirth with business
  deftly blending,
Its heel he's neatly mending—his stool a mossy stone
And his voice has mirth and music in its tone,
Music such as fairy voices own."
  —J. L. Forest. From *Irish Folklore*
    by Rev. John O'Hanlon.

a leprechaun's home

If leprechauns are the descendants of that ancient Irish race, the Tuatha De Danann, the godlike tribe driven underground after the crucial Battle of Moytura, then it seems reasonable to assume that leprechauns may well still live underground.

In his novel *The Crock of Gold*, James Stephens draws for us a modern novelist's imaginative view of a leprechaun's home—and very cosy it is. In the novel, a leprechaun has lured two children, Bridget and Seamus, to his home under a thorn tree. He has done this by teaching the children to play leapfrog with him until their final leap is down a hole which leads to his underground house.

This is how Stephens describes the incident:

"When the children leaped into the hole at the foot of the tree, they found themselves sliding down a dark, narrow slant which dropped them softly into a little room. This room was hollowed out immediately under the tree and great care had been taken not to disturb any of the roots which ran here and there through the chamber in the strangest crisscross fashion. To get across such a place one had to walk around, jump over, and duck under the roots perpetually. Some of these roots had formed themselves very conveniently into long seats and narrow uneven tables, and at the bottom all the roots ran into the floor and away again in the direction required by their business.

"After the clear air outside, this place was very dark to the children's eyes, so that they could not see anything for a few minutes, but after a little time their eyes became accustomed to the semi-obscurity and they were able to see quite well. The first things that they became aware of were six small men who were seated on low roots. They were all dressed in tight green clothes and little leather aprons, and they wore tall green hats which wobbled as they moved. They were all busily engaged making shoes. One was drawing out wax ends on his knee, another was softening pieces of leather in a bucket of water, another was polishing the instep of a shoe with a piece of curved bone, another was paring down a heel with a short broad-bladed knife, and another was hammering wooden pegs into a sole. He had all the pegs in his mouth, which gave him a wide-faced, jolly expression, and according as a peg was wanted he blew it into his hand and hit it twice with his hammer, and then he blew another peg with the right end uppermost, and never had to hit it more than twice. He was a person well worth watching."

michael o' sullivan and the friendly leprechaun

Michael John O'Sullivan was an orphan boy who lived all alone in a small village in the west of Ireland. Every morning he set out along the roads of Galway with his cart full of turf, trying to earn a living to keep him out of the workhouse. But Michael John was not the usual sort of boy. He was shy and never played with other children of his age. Instead, all his spare time was spent reading the old bits of books that he used to pick up on his travels. At night, as he read by candlelight, he would dream of making his fortune and of the day he would be able to give up his turf-round, buy a big house, and live in peace surrounded by beautiful books.

Now, he had read all about leprechauns and the secrets of their gold, and he thought to himself, "While I'm travelling the roads selling my turf, I'll keep my eyes peeled for a leprechaun and my ears cocked for the click-click of his little hammer. If I can catch him and find his crock of gold, I'll be rich for ever."

One summer's evening he was returning from the peat bog, when he saw a movement in the long grass by the side of the road. Jumping off his cart, he dived into the grass. His fingers closed around something live, and he pulled it out. Lo and behold, he was looking into the gasping red face of a little man in a green suit.

"Now I have ye!" said Michael John, "And I'll not let ye free 'til ye tell me where to find your hidden gold."

"God between us and all harm," panted the leprechaun. "Is a man not entitled to a bit of peace and quiet nowadays, or is he to be continually pestered by young and old, and they after his few bob? Easy now with your squeezing, for you're crushing my pipe into the small of my back."

Now Michael John was a kind lad, so he loosened his grip and placed the leprechaun up on

the driving seat of his cart where he could see him better. The little man sat there dusting himself down while Michael John told of his misfortunes, and of his dreams.

The leprechaun took out his pipe and filled it and lit it and re-lit it. Every now and then his shrewd eyes would search the boy's face in an effort to see if the young fellow was telling the truth.

When Michael John was finished, the leprechaun took the pipe from his mouth, cleared

his throat, and said, "Well, Michael John, you're a lucky lad and no mistake. You're either a most deservin' fellow or a terrible liar, and I'm betting you're honest. I'll tell ye what I'm going to do. There's shockin' rumours abroad that we leprechauns is fierce mean and I'm goin' to squash that thunderin' libel for all time. Jump up here beside me and I'll take ye to the fort at Carraroe for that's where I've my gold hid. But we'll want to be quick for we must get there before the sun sets."

Up jumped Michael John beside the leprechaun. The little man took the reins and drove so recklessly that the leprechaun lifted a yard into the air at every pothole. In five minutes flat, they arrived at the fort just as the last rays of orange sun lit the western ocean.

Scarcely had the cart skidded to a halt than the leprechaun leaped off like a scalded cat. He ran towards the fort, shouting over his shoulder, "Quickly now, me young friend, follow me."

Michael John ran after him and entered the fort

through a narrow crack in the rock. Inside, it was pitch black, save for the roof which was streaked with sunlight.

"What are ye standin' round for?" snapped the leprechaun. "There's the gold in that crock. Hurry up, ye've only a few minutes."

Michael John's eyes searched the gloom frantically and finally spotted a large crock in the dim light. He ran over to it and dipped in his hand. A metallic clink was heard, and when he lifted one piece up to his face to examine it, he said aloud, "Solid gold pieces! I'm rich for life!"

"Ye might be dead as well," snapped the leprechaun, "for ye've two more minutes to stow your gold before the sun sets and the fort slams shut. Then ye'll be shut in here 'til kingdom come."

The crock was too wide to take out of the narrow entrance, so Michael John stuffed his four pockets and his cap with the gold coins. It was now pitch black inside the fort, so he rushed for the exit. It was well he did, for just as he felt the fresh breeze on his face, the entrance rock slammed shut and Michael John was left standing on the chilly hillside. There was no sign of the leprechaun.

For the rest of his life, the orphan boy had no worries. He bought his big house and he covered the walls with books from floor to ceiling. He never saw the leprechaun again but he remembered him every night when preparing for bed. As he undressed, he would reach into his pockets to empty them, for Michael John was very tidy. And every night, he would find his pockets mysteriously full of shiny gold pieces.

the leprechaun and the red garters

It was Bank Holiday Monday and the sun was splitting the stones as Tom Fitzpatrick sauntered along on the sunny side of the hedge. He was ruminating on a few little money troubles, but the fine weather was lifting his heart. Indeed, he was just about to try a blast of a song when he heard a clattering sort of noise coming from over the hedge.

"Glorio, Glorio," says he to himself. "It's a bit late in the season for the stonechats to be singing."

Full of curiosity, Tom stole forward on tiptoe into the field so as not to frighten the birds away.

As he rounded the hedge the noise stopped, but there, amid a clump of foxgloves, what did he spy but a brown pitcher! As he stood watching, a wee bit of a man with a little cocked hat strolled over to the pitcher, lifted it to his mouth, took a long draught, and, laying it down, wiped his dripping mouth with his little green sleeve.

"The right man, in the right place, at the right time," said Tom to himself. "Sure a leprechaun can solve all money worries with his gold, and, unless I'm very much mistaken, this here is a leprechaun."

The little man sat down on a little stool nearby and was proceeding to fix a heel on a tiny shoe, just big enough for himself. Tom strolled over and engaged the leprechaun in conversation.

"God bless the work, neighbour."

The leprechaun squinted and said, "Thank you, kindly."

"I wonder you'd be working on the holiday?" said Tom.

"That's my business, not yours," was the answer.

"Well maybe you'll be civil enough to tell me what you've got in the pitcher there?" said Tom.

"That I will with pleasure," said the leprechaun. "It's a nice drop of beer to whet my whistle as I work."

"Where did you get it?" said Tom suspiciously, for he kept a keg of beer himself in his house just down the road.

"By God Almighty," said the leprechaun, "but you're full of old questions. What's in the pitcher? Where did I get it? Why am I working? Maybe, ye'd like to hop into me skin and live me life for me? I'll tell ye what it is. You would be better employed looking after your father's farm than bothering decent people with your foolish questions. Go away with ye now. Your cows are in agony beyond in the barn bursting with milk."

Now Tom was a fine big strapping fellow and he didn't see why he should suffer the rantings of this little scallion. So, he reached suddenly and grabbed the leprechaun and, looking very fierce, he roared, "By the holy, but you've plenty of lip for a small man and I'm telling you direct—if ye don't bring me this instant to your golden store, I'll have your guts for garters this night."

"Simmer down, me bucko, simmer down!" said the leprechaun. "Sure I was only joking and I judged you for a man with a sense of humour. I'll lead you to my gold and you can take your fill and welcome, only loosen your hold or I'll surely burst."

Tom set off across the field as directed, holding the struggling leprechaun under his arm. It was a long journey of five Irish miles over ditch, through briar, over stream, under barbed wire, through bog and swamp, for the little man, out of pure mischief, seemed to choose the most difficult way.

Poor Tom was soon sweating, and bleeding from a number of scratches. But every time he asked, "Is it much further?" the leprechaun giggled and said, "We're just there now. Will ye have a bit of patience?"

At last they came to a large field full of ragweed. The leprechaun pointed to a big plant and said, "Dig under that piece of ragweed and two feet down you'll find a great crock of golden guineas."

"How do I dig when I've no spade, ye silly little man?" exclaimed Tom.

"Sure you've hands like shovels, ye great big gorm," jeered the little man. "Look, I'll do ye a favour for I'm sort of fond of fellows like you with little between their ears. Run home as quick as your legs can carry ye and fetch a spade. I'll tie your garter round this ragweed so ye'll have no difficulty locating it on your return. Now, off with ye!"

The Leprechaun and the Red Garters

Tom didn't wait for a second bidding. He ran home, grabbed a spade, and arrived back in the field sometime later, panting heavily. There was no sign of the leprechaun but a strange sight met his eyes. Every ragweed in the large field (and there were thousands) was decorated with a cute red garter.

molly murphy and the scorched leprechaun

It is a well-known fact in Ireland that leprechauns can be very nasty to people who offend them. They have a vicious streak when they are aggravated, particularly by selfish humans, as the following tale reveals.

John Joe Murphy was a farmer who lived with his cranky wife Sarah about seven miles from Limerick, on the Ennis Road. They had a daughter of ten years, who was quite spoiled, and cranky like her mother. The daughter's name was Molly: 'Molly-Coddle' they called her at school, because she always wanted her own way and was very easily bored indeed.

One day, Molly was walking home from school in a right old temper and amusing herself by kicking the heads off any mushrooms she happened to spy on the side of the road. Suddenly she heard an angry little voice shout, "For the love of God, will ye stop stampin' on those lovely mushrooms! Do ye not realise that's my dinner you're destroyin'?"

Molly looked up in the direction of the voice and there, looking down at her from behind a stone wall, was a very agitated leprechaun.

Quick as a snake, Molly reached out and grabbed the little man, pulled him over the wall headfirst and held him tight, three inches from her nose.

"Now tell me, you horrid little man," she said, with a delighted squeal, "where am I to find this pot of gold that everybody talks about, eh? Tell me quickly now or it'll be the worst for you."

"I know of no pot of gold," said the leprechaun and he added, with some relish, "and if I did,

you'd be the last wretch I'd tell about it."

"Aha!" said Molly, and a horrible grin spread over her face. "Small and smart with it! We'll soon change your tune for you." And without as much as a 'by your leave', she sets off at a canter along the road, carrying the kicking leprechaun under her oxter.

When Molly got home, both her mother and father were out, so in with her to the kitchen and she laying down the law to the unfortunate leprechaun.

"So you won't tell me where your gold is hid? We'll soon see about that. Boys o boys, but we'll have great sport this day," she chortled.

There was an old black grate in the kitchen and a fine big fire under it, and Molly held the leprechaun around the waist with the fire tongs and placed him on the hot metal of the grate. Of course, it wasn't long till the poor leprechaun felt the heat through his little shoes and began to dance and holler.

"Oh take me off, take me off!" he cried. "Me little shoes are burned to a cinder! You'll find the gold buried at the very spot you found me. Take it, take it and bad cess to ye."

Just then, Molly's mother Sarah came into the kitchen carrying a bucket of turf. When she saw the leprechaun, she let the bucket fall and the turf spilled all over the floor.

"Get yourself and your silly leprechaun out of my kitchen, ye spalpeen!" she roared, and helped them on their way with a kick out the half door. The leprechaun escaped Molly's grip in the excitement and scurried off into the undergrowth. Molly disappeared into an outhouse, found a spade

and headed like a dart for the spot where she'd found the leprechaun. She dug and she dug all night, but not as much as a half-penny did she find.

Molly went home at dawn filthy dirty and got a good skelping from her mother for dirtying her frock.

The following evening, Molly's father, John Joe, was passing the field. He stopped, looked, and scratched his head pensively.

"Be God," says he. "That's middling strange! I could have sworn I'd left that field fallow, but I must be mistaken for there it is freshly dug and ready for sowing."

He was just about to pass on when he heard voices and laughter. Now John Joe was partial to a bit of gossip, so he stopped and listened silently and could soon make out a voice saying: "That cranky girl had a hard time of it. Diggin' away all night in vain for my crock of gold. Little did she know it's quite safe down at the old quarry. But whoever gets it must go of a dark night at twelve o'clock and beware that he bring his wife with him."

John Joe went home a thoughtful man and told his wife Sarah all about it and vowed he would go that very night.

"Be sure and stay in tonight, woman, for if you go out ye'll spoil everything."

"Now," thought his wife, when John Joe had gone. "If I could only take the short cut and get to the quarry before him, I would have the pot of gold all to myself, while if that stupid man of mine gets it, I will have nothing." And with that, she went out, ran like the wind, and reached the quarry first. She began to creep down the side of the quarry in the black dark, but there were lots of stones on the path and Sarah slipped and slipped and slipped, until she landed in a heap at the bottom.

And there poor Sarah lay, groaning, for her leg had been broken in the fall.

Just then, her husband arrived at the top of the quarry and began to descend gingerly in the pitch black. He was halfway down when he heard the low groans.

"Cross of Christ about us," he exclaimed, "What is that growling shape down there in the bowels of the earth? Are you evil or are you good? Speak, for I'll go no further!"

"Get yourself down here ye ould fool and help me," cried his wife.

"Is it you that's in it, wife?" asked John Joe. "Didn't I tell you to stay indoors this night?"

At that moment, a peal of hearty laughter split the darkness. This was followed by a merry little song which ended with the ditty:

> *"Folk who are narky, not to mention sarky,*
> *Won't get the gold, 'cause they're far too bold."*

"It was a bad night's work," thought John Joe, as he carried his groaning wife home through black wind and rain, and his humour wasn't improved when he stumbled into his house to find hundreds of mushrooms growing out of his bed!

Oh! It doesn't pay to annoy a leprechaun.

the leprechaun, or fairy shoemaker

Little Cowboy, what have you heard,
Up on the lonely rath's green mound?
Only the plaintive yellow bird
Sighing in sultry fields around,
Chary, chary, chary, chee-ee!
Only the grasshopper and the bee?
"Tip-tap, rip-rap,
Tick-a-tack-too!
Scarlet leather sewn together,
This will make a shoe.
Left, right, pull it tight;
Summer days are warm;
Underground in winter,
Laughing at the storm!"
Lay your ear close to the hill.
Do you not catch the tiny clamour—
Busy click of an elfin hammer,
Voice of the Leprachaun singing shrill
As he merrily plies his trade?
He's a span
And a quarter in height.
Get him in sight, hold him tight,
And you're a made
Man!

You watch your cattle the summer day,
Sup on potatoes, sleep in the hay;
How would you like to roll in your carriage.
Look for a duchess's daughter in marriage?
Seize the Shoemaker—then you may!
"Big boots a-hunting,
Sandals in the hall,
White for a wedding-feast,
Pink for a ball.

This way, that way,
So we make a shoe;
Getting rich every stitch,
Tick-tack-too!"
Nine-and-ninety treasure-crocks
This keen miser-fairy hath,
Hid in mountains, woods, and rocks,
Ruin and round-tow'r, cave and rath,
And where the cormorants build;
From times of old
Guarded by him;
Each of them fill'd
Full to the brim
With gold!

I caught him at work one day, myself,
In the castle-ditch where foxglove grows,—
A wrinkled, wizen'd, and bearded Elf,
Spectacles stuck on his pointed nose,
Silver buckles to his hose,
Leather apron—shoe in his lap—
"Rip-rap, tip-tap,
Tick-tack-too!
(A grasshopper on my cap!
Away the moth flew!)
Buskins for a fairy prince,
Brogues for his son,—
Pay me well, pay me well,
When the job is done!"
The rogue was mine, beyond a doubt.
I stared at him; he stared at me;
"Servant, Sir!" "Humph!" says he,
And pull'd a snuff-box out.
He took a long pinch, look'd better pleased,
The queer little Leprechaun;
Offer'd the box with a whimsical grace,—
Pouf! he flung the dust in my face,
And, while I sneezed,
Was gone!

—*William Allingham*

the pooka: what is it?

The folklore of every nation has its nightmare character, its monster, its fear figure. The Pooka is the bogeyman of Irish Folklore. The name *Pooka* comes from the Gaelic word *Poc*, which means *goat*.

The Pooka does sometimes assume the shape of a goat, but not always. He is often a horse, a bull, or some other huge hairy creature. At other times he is invisible and you only sense his presence by a gust of wind perhaps, or a mysterious howl.

Mr Douglas Hyde, a noted Irish folklorist, describes the Pooka thus:

"Out of a certain hill in Leinster, there used to emerge as far as his middle, a plump, sleek, terrible steed, who spoke in human voice to each person around November Day, and he used to give intelligent answers to such as consulted him concerning all that would happen in the world in the coming year. The people used to leave gifts for him at this hill so that he would not harm them."

So the Pooka rises like a volcano from a hill, he is horse-like and he foretells the future. In stories, he is usually a hairy beast. He steals up from behind and whisks you off on a nightmarish journey over the earth, oceans and heavens. The ride on his back is not thrilling but frightening and you wonder will you ever again step on Mother Earth. If you do, you are a different person in mind and body and you would never wish to repeat the excursion.

BRAVE O'KENNEDY and the pooka

In the townland of Lackeen in the county of Tipperary, there stands a fine old castle in an almost perfect state of preservation. In olden times it was the country seat of the Lords of Ormond and, in particular, the home of 'Brave' O'Kennedy. Now, 'Brave' was so called because he was courageous to the point of insanity and lively with it.

'Brave' was a young squire who lived in his castle with a clatter of brothers and a couple of dozen servants in the days of old. He loved enjoying himself and he insisted that his friends and all his neighbours enjoy themselves with him. Fierce popular he was. He and his brothers spent their days roaming the county for any wee bit of fightin', huntin', racin', fishin', shootin' and general diversion, and sure there's no harm in enjoyin' themselves as young gentlemen with money are wont to do. They had dinners and balls and parties every week and seldom got to the bed before the cock had retired with laryngitis.

But for all the high livin', O'Kennedy was a topping Master and there wasn't one of the servants that hadn't a story to tell of his kindness and his generosity. "He was a lively rogue but a lovely rogue," said his old retainers, and "'twas well known that he'd give a passing beggar the shirt off his back."

Popular therefore he might have been, but it wasn't long before he was famous too, for he did the bravest thing that could be done in those dangerous old times. He stood up to the Pooka. This very night, around the firesides of Tipperary, children sit wide-eyed listening to the tale and they face the dark stairs to bed the braver for its telling.

The tale goes like this. The 'Brave' O'Kennedy was beyond in Eglish churchyard one evening, attending the funeral of an old lady, and afterwards he dined with his cousin next door in Ballyhough Castle. Later, he was riding back home on his thoroughbred hunter Cock-o'-the-Walk and raisin' sparks on the cobbles of the road that led past the church where the corpse was laid.

As he passed, he spotted the light of a candle glimmerin' through the church window and when he drew up, he thought he heard a pair of old women within, talking very loudly. Down he leapt from Cock-o'-the-Walk and pressed his nose close to the window and what do ye think he saw but the pair of old crones sittin' beside the old lady's coffin and the lid off. Inside the coffin lay the corpse that was buried that day. The two crones were in the act of strippin' a fine necklace and a pair of gold rings from her fingers.

"Would ye look at those witches!" says the 'Brave' O'Kennedy. "Is nothing sacred? Had they never a mother themselves, the heartless creatures?" and without more ado, he leaps through the window, showerin' splinters all over the women. I don't know who got the bigger shock—the two women or Cock-o'-the-Walk, but out they ran and O'Kennedy after them, raisin' blue murder and red murder as well.

The two women reached the sanctuary of a high bank opposite the church door where they turned and faced O'Kennedy, shaking their bony fists and shouting.

"Pooka, Pooka," roared one. "Rise up and take that interferin' lout O'Kennedy away to the banks of the Red Sea."

"Leave the scamp there to rot, so he might leave us honest women alone to mind our own business," screamed the other.

Brave O'Kennedy and the Pooka

At their screams, lo and behold, up jumps a big hairy shape from the bottom of a ditch, with his red eyes and nostrils flamin' fire. "I'll get ye, O'Kennedy," says he, "and ye'll rue the day ye interfered in the ancient Church of Eglish, fine fellow as ye think ye are!"

"Ye're a fine big ugly lump of a fellow yourself," says O'Kennedy, drawing his blade from his scabbard. "But ye don't look too intelligent, God bless ye, and I'm thinkin' ye'll need a little more than muscle and bravado to escape the sword of 'Brave' O'Kennedy."

No sooner said than done, O'Kennedy slashed his sword right across the beast's fore feet, sending the creatures front hoofs flying through the air.

"Now maybe ye'll surrender," says O'Kennedy, "for ye can't run any more, I'll be bound."

Instantly, O'Kennedy took off his belt and strapped the remaining legs of the beast snugly. He hauled the package up on his back with as much ease as if the Pooka was a hare or a partridge, for O'Kennedy was powerful strong, I can tell ye. The Pooka kicked, turned and lashed out to no avail. He cursed awful, for he was mad as a hatter, but in spite of his protests he was carried away by 'Brave' O'Kennedy who mounted Cock-o'-the-Walk.

Away with them both along the moonlit bohereens, thundering along with the Pooka roarin' tremendous loud, until O'Kennedy arrived before his own castle walls. Lamps were still lit in the castle for the servants were up expecting the master home, but they were astonished surely to hear the beast bellowing and spitting fire behind his back.

"Open up and let me in," says O'Kennedy, "for I have the Pooka behind me in the saddle and I mean to thrust him down that dark murderin' hole in the castle and put a big stone over it, like a cork in a bottle of whisky."

"If yez dare to do so, boys," shouts the Pooka, "yez'll rue it to the day of your death—and that won't be long comin', for I'll set the castle of Lackeen in a blaze with my breath from foundation to parapet this night. So let O'Kennedy beware what he orders his servants to do."

"Open the gate, Porter," says O'Kennedy, mighty commanding – like. "Who do you obey around here? Your Master or this hairy ould villain?"

"Be God, Master," says the servant, "never let it be said a servant feared to do the bidding of an O'Kennedy in Lackeen. But Master, for mercy's sake, put that horrible howling monster somewhere without the castle, or never the wink of sleep ye'll get this night."

"Ye're right, Tim O'Mara," says O'Kennedy, and there and then he unbuckled the Pooka.

"Get out of my sight, ye unfortunate beast!"

Brave O'Kennedy and the Pooka

says O'Kennedy. "Go off and make toast in
another parish, for if ye hinder me or mine again,
I'll sweep the few remainin' feet from under ye."

So saying, O'Kennedy gave the Pooka a skelp of
the strap across the backside which could be heard
up in Malin Head.

Often towards evening, there is a great Pookawn
goat seen lurking about the castle of Lackeen. I've
my own suspicions the old Pooka may be hid
under his crooked horns and hairy skin, so any
little children that may be out around November's
Eve better keep their eyes skinned for that devil.
That's all I'll say now.

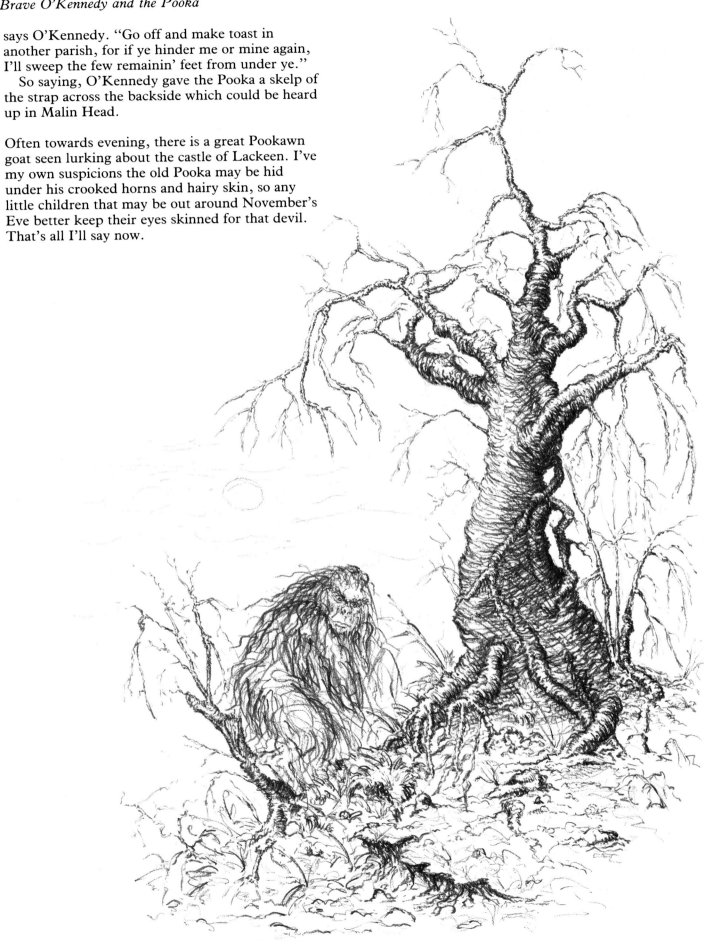

the kildare pooka

Sir Henry Robertson had a grand house on the Dublin-Kildare border. God be good to him, the poor man is long dead but the house still stands and lives. He had a houseful of servants while he lived and they kept the place going even though Sir Henry was often absent across the water on business. With the Master away so often, the servants had the house to themselves a good deal and they used to be frightened out of their lives in the dead of night by strange sounds from the kitchen: banging of doors, clattering of fire irons, pots, pans, dishes and cutlery. When they came down the next morning, the kitchen would be empty, with no sign of an intruder save that the flagstones would be shining clean and the dresser gleaming with polished delph.

One evening, the servants sat up late in the kitchen, keeping one another in heart telling stories about ghosts and strange happenings. There were so many of them crowded round the roarin' fire that the little scullery boy (who slept over the horses in the barn) couldn't find room, so he crept into the warm hearth and fell asleep.

As the small hours came, one by one the servants went off to their beds, forgetting all about the sleeping child. He was awakened by the slam of the kitchen door and the clattering of a donkey's hoofs on the flags. He peeped out and what should he see but a big grey donkey, and he sitting down yawning before the fire.

After a while the Pooka (for that is what it must have been) began scratching his ears in a tired manner, sighed and spoke.

"Sure if I don't start, I'll never finish!" says he.

The poor boy's teeth began to chatter in his head, for he thought, "Now, he's surely goin' to ate me!"

But the fellow with the long ears and tail on him had something else to do. The Pooka stood up on his hind legs, poked the fire to get a blaze going,

then brought in a pail of water from the yard pump. He filled a huge pot with the water and placed it on the fire to boil. Then he put his hand—I mean his hoof—into the hot hearth and pulled the little boy out. The boy roared with fright, but the Pooka only looked at him, thrust out his lower lip to show how little he valued him, and, without more ado, pitched the boy on to a fireside seat.

The boy lay there afraid to move and saying nought, for it seemed the Pooka was in no mood for conversation. He lay down before the fire until he heard the water coming to the boil, and there wasn't a plate, dish or spoon that the Pooka didn't throw into the cauldron. He washed and dried and polished the lot and returned them to the dresser in neat rows. Then he took the broom and gave a good sweepin' to the floor, leaving it all spick and span like a new pin. After that, he came over and sat beside the boy, letting down one of his ears and cocking up the other, and giving the boy a grin. Then, up on his hind legs, he walked out, giving such a slap to the door that the boy thought the house couldn't help tumblin' down.

Well, if there wasn't a hullabaloo next morning when the poor boy told his story. They could talk of nothing else the whole day. One said one thing, another said another, but a fat lazy scullery maid by the name of Kate said the wittiest thing of all.

"Be Dad," says Kate, "if the Pooka has the mind to come in at night and do all the cleanin' and washin', why would we be slavin' ourselves into a sweat during the day?"

"Them's the wisest words you ever said, Kate," said Michael, the stable boy. "And sure, if I could ever have a word with this Pooka, maybe I could ask him to muck out my stables, while he's at it?"

So said, so done. Not a bit of a plate or dish saw a drop of water that day, and crumbs and scraps were let pile up on the floor and everyone went to bed early after sundown.

Next morning, everything was as fine as fire in the kitchen and the Lord Mayor could have eaten his dinner off the floor. These were happy days for the servants and everything went well until Michael, the foolhardy stable lad, said he would stay up one night and have a chat with the Pooka.

Seated in a corner of the kitchen that night, Michael was startled when the door burst open and in marched the Pooka up to the fire. When the pot was filled and the Pooka lay snug and sleepy before the fire, Michael approached.

"Hello there, Sir!" says he. "And if it's not takin' a liberty, might I ask who you are, and why you are so kind as to come here, night after night, and do the day's cleanin' for the girls of the house?"

"No liberty at all," says the Pooka, scratching his flank with a hind hoof. "You see, I was a servant here in the time of the Squire's father and, bless the mark, I was the laziest rogue that ever was clothed and fed, and done nothing for it. When my time came for the other world, this is the punishment that was laid on me—to come here and labour every night, and then to go out in the cold of dawn. It isn't so bad in the fine weather, but if only you knew what it is to stand with your head between your legs facin' the storm till sunrise on a bleak winter's night! If only I had a warm quilted frieze coat itself to keep the life in me them long nights."

"Ye have a horrid time of it surely," said Michael. "We'll see what we can do for ye in the way of insulation. 'Tis the least we could do to repay you for your labours."

To make a long story short, the next night Michael was present again in the kitchen when the Pooka arrived, and if he didn't delight the poor Pooka with one of the Squire's old coats. The Pooka put his two front legs into the sleeves and Michael gave him a hand to button it up over his belly. The Pooka was thrilled and walked over to the glass to view how he looked.

"Well," says he, "it's a long lane that has no turnin' and I'm much obliged to yourself and your fellow servants. You've made me the happiest Pooka in Ireland, aye, and the warmest. Good night to ye, one and all."

As he was walking out the door, the stable lad cried, "Och! Sure you're not going yet, are ye? How about the washing and the sweeping?"

"Ah well now," said the Pooka, "there's a bit of a problem there. My punishment was to last till I was rewarded for my work. This fine coat is my reward so I'll be takin' my leave of you and thank you kindly. Ye'll see no more of me from this."

No more they did, and right sorry they were for being in such a hurry to reward the ungrateful Pooka.

54

the cold iron spurs
and the pooka

John McHale stood six feet six inches in his stockinged feet and at one time gave stalwart service as anchor man on the Mayo tug o' war team. A craggy tower of a man, he farmed eighty acres at Errismore and was seen by many as Ireland's most eligible bachelor. But then things began to change. Neighbours would look at John coming out from the chapel on a Sunday and shake their heads sadly at the transformation.

"The poor man is failed entirely, sure he's only skin and bone!" the women would whisper in clusters. And the men folk sitting in public houses would nod gravely over their drinks and consider whether John was the unfortunate victim of a disease. This is how the story goes.

One day, John took his horse to the forge to get him shod and when he entered the Smithy didn't recognise him, for he had lost six stones in weight and was stooped and pasty with it.

"What ails ye John at all?" asked the Smith. "For if ye keep going like this you'll scarcely be in it by Christmas."

"I've a devil of a problem, Smithy," said John. "And if I don't find a solution quickly I'm a goner surely. I'm sitting at home every night for the past six months, and just before supper time I hear the sound of hoofs outside in the yard and a voice calling me to go out. When I do go out, there's a thing standing there in the dark. He tells me to jump up on his hairy back and I don't seem to have the will to refuse. Once astride, this Pooka gallops away over all Ireland for the duration of the night and I hangin' on for dear life, helter-skelter. Last night, we visited Bantry Castle, the Giants' Causeway up in Antrim and home by way of Limerick City. If he doesn't give me a rest soon I'll surely die, for I'm as weak as a day old kitten."

"Could be the Pooka, indeed," said the Smithy. "And it's well known there's no sayin', no to that devil. But ye'll die on us if this keeps up and I'm thinkin' I might be able to help you."

So saying, the Smithy took up his hammer and picked out a piece of iron and laid it on the anvil without heating it. He hammered it for two hours until he had made a shiny pair of spurs.

"Listen carefully now, John," said the Smithy. "If the Pooka calls tonight, be wearing these spurs and don't spare using them. Make him go twice as fast as he did before, and you on his back."

John thanked the Smithy and went home when his horse was shod and took the cold iron spurs with him. That night, sure enough, just before midnight, he heard the hoofs of the Pooka outside on the cobbles. Quickly, he put on the spurs and answered the summons. He mounted the Pooka's back and held on tight, digging his spurs into the beast's sides as hard as his legs would permit.

The Pooka went like the wind. Sometimes he was above the clouds, other times skimming the peat bogs, but the journey this night was only half as far as other nights. So hard was John pressing the spurs that he felt sure he was making holes in the Pooka's sides, for they were sharp and the beast bucked at every thrust.

The next night, the thing came outside the house and called out, "I'm here!"

"I'll be out to ye presently," roared John.

"Are ye wearin' the sharp spikes tonight?" asked the voice.

"I am indeed!" replied John.

"Then stay inside!" said the Pooka. "This was to be your last night alive. Ye may thank the sharp spikes for your escape!"

From that day to this, John McHale grew in strength and it wasn't long before he was back on the tug o' war team, pullin' for Mayo.

the fairies

Up the airy mountain,
Down the rushy glen,
We daren't go a-hunting
For fear of little men;
Wee folk, good folk,
Trooping all together;
Green jacket, red cap,
And white owl's feather!

Down along the rocky shore
Some make their home;
They live on crispy pancakes
Of yellow tide-foam;
Some in the reeds
Of the black mountain lake,
With frogs for their watch-dogs,
All night awake.

High on the hill-top
The old King sits;
He is now so old and grey
He's nigh lost his wits.
With a bridge of white mist
Columbkill he crosses,
On his stately journeys
From Slieveleague to Rosses;
Or going up with music
On cold starry nights,
To sup with the Queen
Of the gay Northern Lights.

They stole little Bridget
For seven years long;
When she came down again,
Her friends were all gone.
They took her lightly back,
Between the night and morrow,
They thought that she was fast asleep,
But she was dead with sorrow.
They have kept her ever since
Deep within the lake,
On a bed of flag-leaves,
Watching till she wake.

By the craggy hill-side,
Through the mosses bare,
They have planted thorn-trees
For pleasure here and there.
If any man so daring
As dig them up in spite,
He shall find their sharpest thorns
In his bed at night.

Up the airy mountain,
Down the rushy glen,
We daren't go a-hunting
For fear of little men;
Wee folk, good folk,
Trooping all together;
Green jacket, red cap,
And white owl's feather!

—*William Allingham*

60

the fir darrig: who is he?

The Fir Darrig appears in many Irish tales and he is an unforgettable character. The term *Fir Darrig* is Gaelic for *Man in Red*, and he is so called because he invariably wears a red coat and a red hat. He is usually old, and sports a long white beard, but he is very fit and lively. There is nothing he likes better than a good ceilidh, where he is always in the thick of it—either playing his pipes or leading the hornpipes and the jigs. He is the same small stature as the leprechaun but there the resemblance ends.

The Fir Darrig will take a liking to a family and move in with them, lodging amidst the rafters in the attic. While he stays, he will keep himself in good cheer by sampling the wine in the cellar, but he will also protect the household from danger or accident. In many stories, the Fir Darrig introduces himself to a household by requesting permission to warm himself at the fire. This is usually granted speedily, for the Fir Darrig does not like to be refused. However, once the family become accustomed to the new lodger, there is never a dull moment, as the Fir Darrig is a great one for jokes. Of course, he has magical powers and he has been known to help humans to escape who have been trapped inside the Fairy World. In addition, he has his three wishes to dispense, and if he likes you they will be granted, for he has the power to make them come true.

The Fir Darrig is a cheerful individual who never sits still for a moment. If he's not engaging in a vigorous game of hop, step and jump, he's tuning up his pipes for a rollicking reel. If he's not playing practical jokes on you, he's offering to make all your dreams come true.

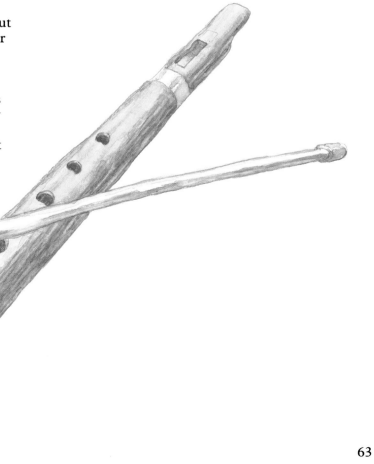

the fir darrig and the black pudding

There is a peat bog in the wilds of Mayo where
only a snipe could nest, and a cold mountain
beside it which casts a shadow even when the
summer sun shines. Here, in a tiny cabin, lived
Fergus O'Hara, his wife Rose and her old mother
Norah – lonely companions who lived life simply,
month after month, with only a rare visit to
Belmullet, the nearest town. January or August,
the rainy Atlantic winds drenched the cabin, while
a few goats, pigs and poultry had a limitless range
over the surrounding hillsides. The family were
frugal. A potato garden and a field of oats were the
sum total of Fergus' tiny harvest. Every Christmas
they killed a pig.

One Sunday evening, at the beginning of winter,
when the day's duties were over, all three sat
chatting before a turf fire that blazed on the
hearthstone. Many family affairs were discussed
and arranged, plans for the coming winter were
formed and meanwhile a small pot of boiling
potatoes foamed white on the fire and a little
dripping slowly simmered in the frying pan. The
table was set for their homely meal.

"Oh, 'tis a hard old life and no mistake, and we one step ahead of the bailiff, Rose," said Fergus to his wife, for if truth be told he seldom addressed any remark to her old mother for fear he'd receive a clout on the butt of the ear. "Oh, I wish to goodness we could have all our own way for a change," says he, "so that we needn't fear the blight nor the rentman!"

No sooner were these words pronounced than a squeaky voice rang out from the rafters above.

"Well Fergus, me old flower, aren't you the lucky man!"

Six startled eyes looked up in the direction of the thatch, and there, sitting on a rafter, was a little man dressed in scarlet with a long white beard, hanging down from the beam. He sat cross-legged like a tailor.

"I'm sayin', ye're in luck this night, Fergus," he continued, "for I've a mind to give ye your wish and I'll give another wish to Rose and one to old Norah. So, cudgel your brains, me darlins, for as ye all know, the Fir Darrig has the power to make all your wishes come true."

With that, he sat back against the thatch with his eyes dancing in his face and his mouth grinning from ear to ear.

"God save us, it's the Fir Darrig!" muttered old Norah, blessing herself. "Sure we'll have no truck with that devil or he'll eat us out of house and home."

Fergus was inclined to agree with his mother-in-law, much as he hated the sensation, but Rose was thinking hard as she sat stoking the fire.

"Well," she said, after a long pause, "if that red fella can grant us all riches, amn't I the sorry woman that I didn't buy that fine hog's pudding I seen last Easter in Kitty Flannagan's shop? I wish I had it fryin' in the pan for our supper this evening."

No sooner said than done. A fine plump black pudding hit the pan with a splash of fat, and in no time at all a delicious odour spread through the cottage.

Fergus looked at the pudding, stood up with a roar and, turning in a passion to his simple wife, cried out, "Ye stupid stump, look what ye've done now! Isn't that a great wish of yours after the chance ye got? Ye have no sense at all to request a wish that will be ate up tonight, and nothing at all left for tomorrow. It's little grey stuff ye have under yer cap!"

He stood looking at his wife in disgust and, as an afterthought, said, "I wish one end of the hog's pudding was stuck to your nose, ye foolish creature."

Immediately, the smoking pudding flew from the pan and fixed itself to the end of Rose's nose.

The poor woman jumped about in an agony of pain, shaking her head vigorously from side to side to try to dislodge the burning meat. She screamed and she roared, for the hot pudding was raising blisters on the top of her nose.

The sight of her daughter in such pain, raised the anger of old Norah. Turning wildly to Fergus, she roared, "Look what ye've done now, ye clumsy bullock! Ye ought to be ashamed of yourself, treatin' your wife like that. I wish the other end of the meat was stuck to your nose. T'would be just reward for ye!"

Now the third wish was spent and quick as lightning the other end of the pudding affixed itself to the bulbous nose of Fergus and he and his wife danced a painful jig around the room, screaming loudly. Pull as they might, the pudding would not come free and the Fir Darrig in the rafters took up his pipes with a cackle of laughter and played in quick succession *The Wind That Shakes The Barley*, *God Speed The Plough*, *Off She Goes*, and *The Humours Of Glinn* – all lively jigs sure to liven up the saddest wake.

Old Norah joined in the dance, trying to pull the hot pudding off their noses but her squeals revealed that she had burned her fingers to the bone and she retired to a corner, blowing on her hands to cool them. All the while, the Fir Darrig kept up the music with a virtuoso performance on the pipes and 'twas well the nearest neighbour was twelve miles distant for they'd surely have called the police with the murdering noises coming from the cabin.

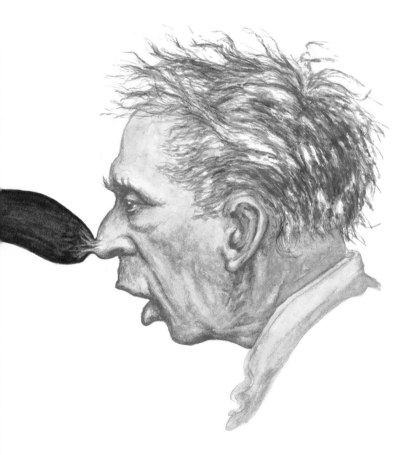

When he'd finished *The Reel Of Three*, the Fir Darrig gathered up his pipes, crowed like a cock and disappeared through the straw in the roof, leaving a gaping hole through which the moon peeped.

Old Norah found a knife and scraped the pudding from the noses of Fergus and Rose leaving marks behind which looked like ringworm. All three of them decided to keep silent about the cause of their injuries but, as often happens, the story got out and was well-known the length and breadth of the parish. On the rare occasions that Fergus and Rose travelled to Belmullet, their old friends would cast secret glances at their noses and reflect on the odd humour of the Fir Darrig and the vanity of human nature.

the fir darrig on night shift

Once upon a time, in a very remote corner of the County Clare there was a boy called Padraig who was the son of a poor farmer. Although he was quite small, he used to help his father at the farm work, for it was a small farm and Padraig's father had little money to spare to employ a farm labourer.

Well, one week strange things started to happen around the farm and the curious thing was that these strange events always seemed to happen at night. Talking, singing and music could be heard in the farmyard and its buildings—and somebody was letting the hens out of their house as in the morning they would be found scattered all around the farm (and looking fairly exhausted at that). But the strangest thing of all was that every morning when the farmer entered his mill, he discovered that all the meal had been ground overnight and was neatly collected in a row of ten sacks.

Padraig decided to investigate these strange happenings. So, one night when his parents were fast asleep, he crept out of the house with an old oil lamp to light his way. Into the mill with him and up to the loft where he hid close to a window and put out his oil lamp. Scarcely had his eyes become accustomed to the moonlight, when there was a ferocious cackling and fluttering of hens down in the yard. Padraig looked out the window and he could scarcely believe his eyes.

Below, six little men in red jackets and hats were jumping around the farmyard playing leapfrog

with the hens. The leader sat on a wall playing lusty tunes on a tin whistle, and all the while his companions whooped and hollered as they leaped over the backs of the bewildered poultry. At the end of a lively jig, the tin whistler suddenly shouted, "Right lads, back to work!" Whereupon, all six Fir Darrigs (for that is what they were) formed up in a line and marched off towards the mill and Padraig.

Now Padraig couldn't prevent a shiver of apprehension when he heard the procession enter the grinding room just below him, but he held his breath, crept behind a barrel and peered through a gap in the planks. As soon as the little men entered the room, they lit torches and set about grinding the meal with a vengeance while the tin whistler, who was acting as foreman, barked orders and regaled the workers with snatches of music.

Padraig kept watching, but what with having to squint through the boards his eyes became heavy and he fell asleep. The next thing he knew it was morning and the mill was silent except for the busy chirping of the birds outside in the trees. When he descended the wooden ladder he noticed that everything was clean and tidy, and there, beside the wall as usual, were the ten full sacks of ground meal.

Every night the work was carried out and soon Padraig's father became very rich, for when he sold the extra sacks of meal he had all the profit to himself. Padraig went often to the mill at night to watch the Fir Darrigs at work and he grew to love their leader, for he worked so hard keeping the workers in order yet had no reward for it and could not apparently afford to replace his tattered clothes by a new suit. Padraig decided to give him a present.

He took out his savings and bought a suit of silk which he thought would fit the Fir Darrig, and one night he left it in the mill and crept up to the loft to watch the proceedings.

It wasn't long before the Fir Darrig found the suit, took it up, fingered it curiously and admired it. Then he dressed himself in it and began to walk up and down the mill, strutting vainly and calling on the others to admire him. When midnight came and the workers went outside for their nightly

game of leapfrog with the hens, the Fir Darrig stayed indoors in case he got his new clothes dirty.

When the workers came back in, sweating and laughing, the Fir Darrig said to them, "Now look here, my good men. Hard work is not for gentlemen and I'm sure you'll agree that in this fine suit, I look every inch a gentleman?" With that he ran out of the mill, followed by all the little workers.

No more meal was ground that night, nor the next, nor the next. Padraig waited some time hoping that his friend would return but he did not. Soon the hens began to rest easy and lay their eggs in peace. Years went by and the boy grew into a fine gentleman himself, for his father had made so much money that he had spent a great deal of it on his son's education.

In time Padraig became engaged to a beautiful maiden, so beautiful that some folk said she must be the daughter of the King of the Fairies; and perhaps she was, for a strange thing happened on their wedding day.

As the guests stood at the banqueting table ready to drink the bride's health, there appeared suddenly in Padraig's right hand, as if by magic, a golden cup filled with wine.

Padraig guessed that it was a gift from the Fir Darrig and without any fear he raised the cup and he and his wife drank from it. No harm came to them through it, only increased happiness and prosperity.

The cup has been passed down from Padraig to his sons and is in the possession of their family to this day.

the Banshee: who is she?

There was one noise in the world that the old noble families of Ireland feared above all. The O'Donnells, the O'Malleys and the O'Gradys all hated the song of the Banshee. Snug in warm castle or cottage, this dreaded music outside meant imminent death to one of the family. When they heard the Banshee, often at dead of night, all hopes faded. If one of the family was old and lay sick in bed, they immediately knew the outcome; if the Banshee's wail was heard when all the household felt hale and hearty, a shiver ran through the company for they knew their fortunes would change and a death could not be avoided.

The Banshee of Irish folklore appears as a beautiful young girl who is thought to be the spirit of a deceased relative who died young and comes back from the grave to warn of death. Her song is piercing and cuts to the heart. Its tone is melancholy and prophetic. Sometimes she appears as an old woman in a funeral shroud. She has long hair streaming in the wind and a pale complexion with eyes red from continual weeping.

Sometimes the Banshee is only heard, not seen. One story tells of an old lady of noble blood lying close to death in her stately castle. One evening, she opened her tired eyes and pointed to the window, a happy smile on her face. Her family around her bedside followed her gaze but could see nothing. Suddenly the room was filled with the sweetest music which seemed to come from the opened window. A search was made in the grounds but nothing human was seen. Yet the music continued all through the night. Next morning the old lady lay dead. The music ceased and all present knew that they had been visited by the Banshee.

The term 'Banshee' (Bean—Woman: Shee—Fairy) means 'The Woman of the Fairy Race' and comes from old Gaelic. She is not human but spirit and has been known to follow a family across the seas should they emigrate. Her sad message has been heard on the Canadian prairies and in the Australian Bush.

Not long ago the O'Grady family from County Limerick sold their ancestral holding and moved to Red Deer, Alberta. They worked hard and prospered and within twenty years were the proud owners of many acres in their new land. They had long forgotten the old stories they had learned at an Irish fireside.

One winter's night Thomas O'Grady, his wife Margaret and son Sean passed the time in their Canadian home playing cards. When they heard the strange sad singing outside they looked at each other in puzzlement as their farmhouse was isolated. They said nothing but continued their game. As the music came closer long-forgotten memories of old fairy lore rose to the surface of their minds. Margaret thought she saw a shadow pass the window, but when her husband and son went out to investigate they found nothing. Yet still the moaning song continued. They went to sleep with little difficulty as they had long since rejected the idea of Banshees.

Next morning Thomas and Sean went fishing on the lake, a pleasure they permitted themselves now and again. When they failed to return at the usual time for dinner, the alarm was raised and the lake shore searched. At exactly the hour when the Banshee's cry had been heard the previous evening, a group of men were seen approaching the farmhouse. They bore with them the drowned bodies of Thomas and Sean.

Margaret O'Grady once more believes in Banshees.

Here are some verbatim reports from country people who have experienced her fatal warning.

"I heard the Banshee crying not long ago, and within three days a boy of the Murphy's was killed by his own horse as he was bringing his cart to Kinvara. I would have stood barefooted in the snow listening to the tune she had, so nice and so calm and so mournful. I had a daughter in America and she came home. As she was coming into the house, I heard the Banshee keening and I had a dream of my daughter stretched out as a corpse on a table. The keening continued until twelve o'clock that night. Within a short time that daughter was dead and it was on my own table she was stretched as a corpse."

—*Old Simon*

"Crying for those that are going to die you'd hear of often enough. And when my own wife was dying, the night she went, I was sitting by the fire, and I heard a noise like the blow of a flail on the door outside. And I went to see what it was, there was nothing there. But I was not in any way frightened and wouldn't be if she came back in a vision, but glad to see her I would be."

—*A. Herd*

"I heard the Banshee and saw her. I and six others were card playing in the kitchen at the big house, that is sunk into the ground, and I saw her up outside of the window. She had a white dress and it was if held over her face. They all looked up and saw it, and they were all afraid and went back but myself. Then I heard a cry that did not seem to come from her but a good way off, and then it seemed to come from herself. She made no attempt to twist a mournful cry but all she said was 'Oh-Oh, Oh-Oh', but it was as mournful as the oldest of the old women could make it that was best at crying the dead."

—*O. King*

"There was a man near us that was ploughing a field, and he found an iron box, and they say there was in it a very old Irish book with all the knowledge of the world in it. Anyway, there's no question you could ask him, he couldn't answer. And what he says of the Banshee is, that it's Rachel mourning still for every innocent of the earth that is going to die, like as she did for our Lord when the king had like to kill him."

—*John Cloran*

the Banshee who washes red clothes in the moonlight

In The Ulster Cycle of early Irish stories, an incident is told concerning Cuchulainn, the Hound of Ulster, who was walking out one day with Cathbad when they came to a ford on a river. There they saw a young girl, white-skinned and fair-haired, washing and wringing out clothes on the bank of the stream. The garments were stained crimson red and the beautiful girl was crying and keening all the time. Cathbad turned to Cuchulainn and said, "Little Hound, do you see what that young girl is doing? It is your red clothes she is washing. She is crying as she washes because she knows you are going to your death against Maeve's great army."

— *Cuchulainn of Muirthemne*

The sixteenth century castle of that great Irish warrior Shane O'Neill lies on the banks of Lough Neagh in the northern province of Ulster. Today it is a sorry ruin, but at the beginning of this century it still showed a light at night and was the comfortable home of the great man's descendants. A strange thing happened there when Sir Richard and Lady Fanworth visited the castle to spend a day or two with their old friends Cormac and Cait O'Neill.

The Fanworths arrived before the castle at dusk and were somewhat saddened to observe that a fire had destroyed part of the castle and that their hosts, lacking the finance to affect repairs, were confined to living in one wing while the remainder of the fine residence was usurped by weed and vermin. The old moat, which had surrounded the castle, was partly filled in and had grown into a pitiful marsh while a few thin sheep cropped a once-cobbled courtyard.

However, despite the dismal exterior, the welcome from their hosts was full and warm and it was pleasurable to sit over a fine meal of salmon and quail, enhanced by a fine claret which their gracious hosts had saved for such an occasion. The table conversation was jovial and genuine, for Cormac and Cait were the best of hosts, until Lady Fanworth asked, "And how is Maeve?" referring to the young daughter of the house. "Why, she must be twenty by now?"

"And a beautiful young lady, I'll be bound," added Sir Richard. "I remember her as a very pretty child."

The talk came to a standstill and there was a long nervous lull in the conversation while Cormac looked at his wife and Cait herself stared silently at the tablecloth. Sir Richard, anxious to spare his hosts any embarrassment, turned the conversation to easier matters and soon the happy party feeling was restored. It was with great good humour that Sir Richard and Lady Fanworth retired for the night to the guest room overlooking the moat.

What with the travelling and the heavy meal, both were soon sleeping peacefully, but Lady Fanworth came awake with a start in the small hours. As she lay there in the dark, she became aware of a white light outside and singing from a beautiful voice carried to her through the night. Quietly, so as not to wake her husband, she crept to the window and peered out. There below, at the edge of the moat, knelt a woman clearly visible in the moonlight. She was old but her voice had the

tone of a girl and her song was the saddest ever heard. As she sang, she washed a red petticoat in the moat's muddied waters—one could see it was red for the area round the woman was strangely bright.

Lady Fanworth thought she met the woman's gaze for some seconds, but no recognition was registered and the singing and washing continued for a full two minutes or longer. Suddenly, all was silent again. The form vanished and with it, the light. Lady Fanworth returned to her bed, but she never closed an eye till dawn streaked the eastern sky.

Next morning while dressing, Lady Fanworth related the night's events to her bemused husband and, rather than keep it to himself, he raised the matter with much humour over breakfast with his hosts.

"My good wife," he began, "tasted a little too much claret last night, I fear. During the night she swears she saw O'Neill's Banshee washing clothes in your moat." He laughed heartily, but neither Cormac nor Cait smiled.

"It wasn't the claret, Sir Richard," said Cait quietly.

Cormac O'Neill cleared his throat and said, "Our daughter Maeve died a week ago in a hunting accident, and each night since the Banshee sings at the moat."

Sir Richard and Lady Fanworth left for home that day before lunch.

O'CARROLL'S
BANSHEE

Gerard O'Carroll was a mountain of a man with a face like granite and the temper of a spitting cat. He was a man of thirty years at the time of this tale and, as local chieftain, well used to getting his own way. If you were to visit Lough Derg today you would see the ruins of Terryglass Castle, once the family home of the O'Carrolls. Lough Derg is on the Shannon and is the lower of that river's lakes; O'Carroll's castle stands on its eastern shore, the waters lapping at its base.

It was a huge castle, with bulging bastions at each corner, but the wind and the rain of many centuries have reduced its height and, although stairways of stone and interior walls are still clearly visible, clumps of grass sprout from wall and floor alike.

The castle rests on a limestone platform. On three sides, as far as the eye can see, rich farmland reaches to the horizon, and on the fourth lies the lake, calm as a bowling green in summer, but subject to sudden squalls and mysterious currents in other seasons.

Here Gerard O'Carroll lived his life, monarch of all in the barony and surrounded day and night by countless retainers. Each evening Gerard sat at table with family, friends and guests, and the sweet aroma of roasting meat, mulled wine and scented ladies was as a sauce to the lively conversation. The huge banquet was followed by singing and dancing and often it was dawn before tired bodies reached soft beds.

One particular night, when the harper had plucked his last chorus and the household was

preparing to retire for the night, the chieftain gave orders for the forester, the huntsman and two stalwart clansmen to be ready next morning at an early hour on the banks of Lough Derg. It was his intention to row over to the other side of the lake to visit another chieftain, Edwin O'Brien.

Fair enough. The morning started well, the sun rose bright and the day was perfectly calm as they set out, rowing hard, across the shimmering surface of the wide lake. Faithful servants followed the boat with their eyes till it was a speck on the horizon, for they were fond of their master despite his temper and they knew his heart was gold. O'Carroll was not expected to return until the following evening and the household felt lost that night as they sat in the great hall, now silent, and talked of all the great feasts and fun they had enjoyed over the years.

Later that evening, while the warders prepared for their nightwatch, a loud piercing scream was heard coming over the water of Lough Derg. It froze the hearts of all who heard it, such was its

strength and painful tone. All who were fit rushed to the ramparts and searched the black darkness trying to locate the cause. Just then, the moon came from behind the clouds and the watching battlements beheld a terrifying sight. Across the glassy surface of the lake moved a beautiful female figure, clad in white with long flowing locks. She did not seem to touch the water but glided towards the castle and as she drew near, the dreadful wail grew louder and more urgent. Many a heart beat faster as the apparition passed the ramparts and moved down the lake trailing her dreadful song in her wake until at last it died away in the dark distance.

There was consternation on the ramparts.

"It is no doubt O'Carroll's Banshee," cried one.

"I fear some sad accident will soon cause the death of our chief!" said another. Few slept soundly in Terryglass Castle that night.

It took O'Carroll's boat half a day to reach the other side of the lake. When he stepped on to the jetty, Edwin O'Brien and his kinsmen were there to greet him. O'Carroll was brought with great ceremony to O'Brien's castle and spent the afternoon with his hosts hunting in the Slieve Bloom mountains. O'Carroll was in great cheer and no one could match his tally with bow or spear.

That evening at a banquet held in his honour, Edwin praised his guest's hunting skills but finished his address to the assembled company with the dry taunt, "I have never seen hunting skills as powerful as those of our guest but I'll wager he would not be as accurate with sword in battle."

O'Carroll, whose hot temper was roused by the wine, resented this slur and nothing would satisfy him but a duel next morning with an embarrassed Edwin. Mediators tried to calm the dispute but O'Carroll was steadfast. So a sorry company of reluctant combatants assembled before dawn on the lawn before O'Brien's castle.

At this very moment, the ramparts of Terryglass Castle were lined with worried kindred, scanning the waters, anxiously willing the safe return of their chieftain. The hours passed and at last, towards noon, younger ears picked out a steady booming rhythm crossing the waters. A speck on the horizon slowly materialised into a boat and as it grew nearer, the watchers saw the funeral drums and the bared heads of their kinsmen in the boat. Tears ran freely as the body of O'Carroll was lifted on to the quayside and borne to the chapel. O'Carroll's Banshee had given true warning.

BALOR OF THE EVIL EYE

Balor of the Evil Eye was a famous and fiendish sorcerer in ancient Ireland. Before the Celts and before Christianity, the most famous race to rule Ireland was a godlike people called the Tuatha De Danann (The Tribe of the Goddess Dana). They were a tall handsome people, accomplished in the arts and skilled in magic. The Tuatha De Danann ruled Ireland for close on two hundred years and their sworn enemies during this time were a warlike people called the Fomorians. Balor of the Evil Eye was the Fomorian wizard and leader. Although a giant, Balor was feared even more for his awesome magical powers which were superior to the magic of the Tuatha De Danann. But it was for his eye that he was most feared. Balor had a third eye in the back of his skull, which was usually covered by a metal eye-patch. When this

eye was exposed in battle, it shot forth deadly fire which razed all within its range. There was no protection against such a lethal weapon and Balor of the Evil Eye was considered immortal.

There was another reason for Balor's immortal reputation. His wife, Caithleann, a prophetess, had foretold that her husband could never be slain, save by his own grandson. They had one daughter, Eithne, and in order to protect himself, Balor locked her away so that she could never marry. However she fell in love and had a child. This child was named Lugh and grew into a strong warrior. According to *The Book of the Invasions of Ireland*—one of the earliest manuscripts—it was he who finally ended Balor's villany. Lugh, the grandson, slew Balor, his grandfather, with a sling shot in the second Battle of Moytura while helping the Tuatha De Danann to defeat the Fomorians for the last time.

However, there are several versions of the violent death of Balor and here is one of them.

the downfall of Balor

The rugged landscape of Donegal lay smouldering from the excesses of Balor. Each household had its sad tale to tell—a herd of cattle stolen, a son lost defending the meagre homestead. Balor of the Evil Eye seemed untouchable and frequently he retreated to his impregnable stronghold to plan his next outrage.

But a druid had said that Balor would be killed by his own grandson. Now Balor had only one child, his daughter Eithne, and to prevent complications he imprisoned her in a stone tower on the summit of a rock at the eastern end of windswept Tory island. Guarding her night and day, he placed a dozen matrons and gave them instructions not to let any man near her, nor even to speak of men. Eithne spent many years in this prison and grew up a beautiful woman, but she had dreams of men and often asked about the people she could see passing in boats to the mainland shore.

On the mainland lived three brothers—one was a smith, one was the lord of the district and the third was a soldier. The lord's name was Cian and he owned a precious cow who was such a good milker that she was famous in the district and everybody coveted her. Cian was vigilant and guarded her constantly, but Balor had heard of this cow and had decided to steal her.

One day Cian went to his brother the smith to have some swords fashioned and took the cow with him on the end of a rope. While he was inside the forge, he asked his brother the soldier to mind the cow outside. Balor, using his magic, took the form of a redheaded boy, and offered to mind the cow for the soldier. As soon as he got the halter in hand, Balor carried her off like lightning to his stronghold.

The three brothers were furious when they discovered how they had been tricked and in desperation Cian visited an old druid and asked for his advice. The druid said he would help. He dressed Cian up in lady's clothes and whisked him to Tory island where Eithne lay imprisoned. Cian, disguised as a woman, won access to Eithne and they fell in love, while the twelve matrons were lulled asleep by the druid. Cian remained with Eithne for a week and then returned to his own territory while the waking matrons remembered nothing.

Matters remained like this until the daughter of Balor gave birth to a son. The infant was named Lugh. Balor discovered this and ordered that the grandson be rolled in a sheet which had been fastened with a delg, or pin, and drowned in a whirlpool. But the baby fell from the sheet and was secretly rescued by Cian's brother the smith who raised him and fed him so that he grew up into a very strong man.

Balor thought he was safe again, but his druid told him that it was Cian who had fathered the baby. This put Balor into a terrible rage and he came for Cian, bent on vengeance. Laying the lord's head upon a large white rock, he killed Cian with one stroke of his huge sword. The rock with its red stain is still there today.

The Downfall of Balor

Lugh heard of the horrible murder of his father and vengeance stewed in him until one day Balor visited him in the forge. Now, Balor did not know the smith's boy was his own grandson, so he was at his ease. Stung with fury, Lugh took a glowing rod from the furnace and thrust it through the basilisk eye of Balor. Thus the son avenged his father's murder by slaying his wicked grandfather and executing the fatal decree.

the mystery

I am the wind which breathes upon the sea,
I am the wave of the ocean,
I am the murmur of the billows,
I am the ox of the seven combats,
I am the vulture upon the rocks,
I am a beam of the sun,
I am the fairest of plants,
I am a wild boar in valour,
I am a salmon in the water,
I am a lake in the plain,
I am a word of science,
I am the point of the lance in battle,
I am the God who created in the head the fire

Who is it who throws light into the meeting on
   the mountain?
Who announces the ages of the moon?
Who teaches the place where couches the sun?
                         (If not I)
         —*Translated by Douglas Hyde (1860–1949)*

where did they all come from?

For centuries, Irish people have been telling stories of Leprechauns, Fir Darrigs, Pookas and Banshees, and today they are well-known all round the world. Some people still believe that these characters do exist. A farmer skirts a fairy fort on his tractor, sensing that were he to plough it up bad luck would haunt him. A factory cannot be built on a certain site for an old tree stands there and must not be disturbed lest the fairies be annoyed. Where did these creatures of Irish lore originate; were they characters conjured up in the imaginations of simple peasants? Or were they real people?

The Pooka is surely a spirit—he would be more at home in a nightmare. When he does take a shape, it's usually animal. The Banshee is a restless spirit, returning from beyond the grave, to prophesy death. But the Leprechaun and Fir Darrig are different. They are not the usual fairy. At times, they seem human—they eat, sleep, drink, enjoy human entertainments, and work at human trades. They are small in stature but not tiny and they seem to understand, only too well, human nature. If there are Pygmies in the Congo basin and Bushmen in the Kalahari Desert, why not another race of small men in Ireland?

In his book *Fians, Fairies and Picts*, David MacRitchie maintained the presence of a tiny dwarf race in Scotland long ago. The remains of ancient cave dwellers have been uncovered at Spy in Belgium and a study of the skeletons drew this conclusion from an anthropologist: "These men belonged to a race of small stature . . . having voluminous heads, massive bodies, short arms and bent legs. They led a sedentary life, frequented caves, manufactured flint implements and were contemporary with the mammoth."

An ancient Scottish song recalls a similar creature:

> *"His legs scarce a six-inch length*
> *And thick and thimber was his thigh:*
> *Between his brows there was a span,*
> *And between his shoulders there was three."*

But the most entertaining story of the presence of small-statured men in olden times comes from an old man living in the townland of Drumcrow, County Antrim who, in describing the Picts who used to inhabit Scotland and Ireland, said, "Low set, heavy made people they were, broad in the feet—so that in rain, they could lie down with their feet in the air and shelter."

In addition, their diminutive underground dwelling places and other pre-historic artefacts such as flint arrowheads ("elf-shots"), not to mention the skeletal remains that have been discovered, all point to at least the possibility of Leprechauns as near neighbours of humans—a remnant of a small statured race who had been driven to live in the wilds in low houses half-sunk in the ground.

If the little people are not real, it is a brave man who would say so publicly in certain parts of Ireland today. While there may be many to agree with you in such an opinion, some would react quite nervously, while others would be aggressively opposed to such heresy.

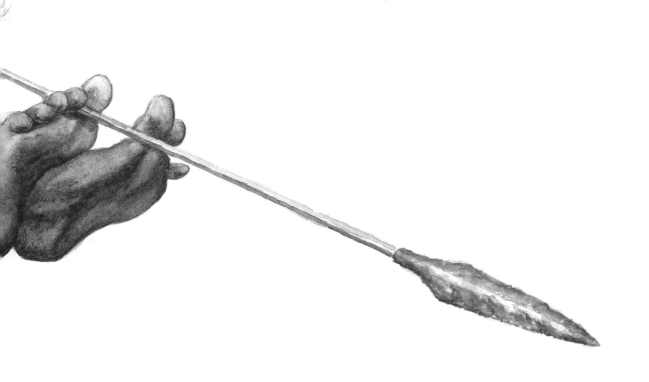

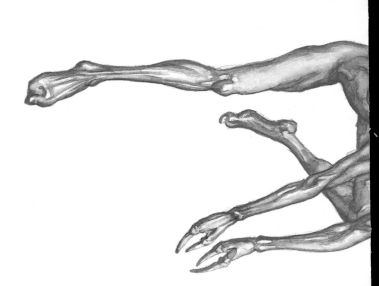

did they come from above?

If you ask some country people who the Leprechauns are, you may be told they are fairies. If you were to ask where the fairies come from, some older people might tell you they come from heaven. There is a strong school of thought supporting the theory that most of the characters of Irish folklore are fallen angels and the explanation runs like this.

108

During the war in heaven between the Almighty and Lucifer, some of the angels remained neutral. When the heavenly battle was settled, God opened the gates of heaven and set about casting out the angels who did not support him and that work went on for forty days and forty nights. As they fell through the atmosphere, some of them stayed in the air and these were represented by the Pooka. Some of them fell on the land and these would include the Leprechauns and the Fir Darrigs. Still more fell in the sea and these became water sprites. This theory went on to say that the Leprechauns, Fir Darrigs and Pookas were partly human and partly spirit and that there is 'not as much blood in them altogether as would drop from the point of a pen.' If it were not that they yearned to return to heaven, they would destroy the world. They were about two-and-a-half feet in height, had red hair, and were very fond of singing, piping and dancing. By all accounts they seldom harmed people unless some unkindness was done to them.

This theory fits in nicely with the basic character of both the Leprechaun and the Fir Darrig. It is also a quite ingenious explanation for the antics of the Pooka.

There is one further theory put forward to explain the origins of these creatures and this will become apparent in the next chapter.

the earliest times in ireland

Ireland is old, very old, and for one reason or another it has not changed much. As I mentioned in my introduction, under the grass of Ireland lies the historic evidence of how people lived thousands of years ago. Even today, archaeological treasures are being uncovered in Ireland for the first time, and let us hope they stay in Ireland, for a country surely owns its own heritage.

When we talk about early settlement in Ireland, we are thinking in terms of thousands of years before Christianity. Exact detail and dating is difficult and guesses are based on tradition, which in turn is dependant on early manuscripts and oral folklore. Many of the earliest manuscripts have been lost. The Celts did not commit their thoughts to writing until the arrival of Christianity in Ireland in the fifth century. So the knowledge of earlier settlement in Ireland is based on tradition to a greater extent, perhaps, than in other lands.

According to the ninth century Annals, the earliest people in Ireland were the *Firbolgs*, although tradition suggests the earlier presence of at least three tribes of Greek origin. The Firbolg (*Fir—Men, Bolg—Bag*) or Bag men were so called because they were thought to have carried bags full of soil to build the great monuments of the East and they also are thought to have been Greek. They were a small straight-haired swarthy race with a reputation for being talkative, guileful, disrupters of councils and assemblies, and great promoters of discord. They had laws and social institutions and a King at the hill of Tara in County Meath. It was the Firbolgs who built the earthen raths, circles and forts which are still intact in Ireland today.

The next invasion of Ireland was by the *Tuatha De Danann* (*Tuatha—Tribe, De Danann—of the goddess Dana*). This tribe were thought to be descended from one of the Greek tribes who had inhabited Ireland in even earlier times and had returned to Greece. The Tuatha De Danann came to Ireland from Greece, having settled for a while in both Scandinavia and Scotland on the way. They were a tall fair race, very strong physically but also skilled in using metals, music, poetry, herbal medicine and magic. When they arrived in Ireland, they challenged the resident Firbolgs and this led to the First Battle of Moytura.

In this great battle, which is thought to have been fought in the Sligo area, the Tuatha De Danann defeated the Firbolgs, although heavily outnumbered. There were many casualties on both sides. The Firbolgs were said to have been finally dispirited by the magical powers of their opponents. In its aftermath, the Firbolgs were a spent force politically, but they blended with the victors to produce a race of people who are the true ancestors of Irish peasant stock.

After some years of peace, the supremacy of the Tuatha De Danann was threatened by old enemies called the Fomorians. The Fomorians have been described as "half-monster, half-human African pirates", and in general got a very hostile press. They were led by the evil magician Balor of the Evil Eye and the confrontation led to the Second Battle of Moytura. This seems to have been even more bloody than the first war against the Firbolgs, and for a long time Balor's evil eye wrecked havoc amidst the ranks of the Tuatha. But the Tuatha De Danann were finally victorious when Lugh, hero of the home warriors, slew Balor by casting a mighty sling-shot which pierced his infamous eye.

The Tuatha De Danann ruled Ireland for two hundred years and during that time their reputations as masters of magic grew. They are also remembered as great masons and they built the stone cairns, duns and cashels of Ireland.

MacFurbis wrote, "Everyone who is fair and vengeful, every plunderer, every professor of music or entertainment, everyone who is adept at druidical and magical arts, is a descendant of the Tuatha De Danann."

The Milesians or the Gaedhil conquered the Tuatha De Danann. At first they were going to destroy them, but instead they banished the Tuatha De Danann to live underground in the less hospitable parts of Ireland. So, the once proud warriors of a great race were forced to excavate homes for themselves in the ground, and here they retired with their magic and mysterious healing powers so that the Gaedhil were induced to consider them elusive spirits.

BRUGh of the BOYNE

The Tuatha De Danann built this famous
underground cavern at New Grange over five
thousand years ago. The structure of the tumulus
is composed of stone wall uprights, with rough
stone slabs providing the roof. There is an inner
and an outer chamber and entrance is by a narrow
doorway through which the dawn sun shines on
the morning of the summer solstice. The inner
chamber can accommodate twenty people
comfortably, and it may well be the oldest
observatory known. The rugged underground
structure is covered with a circular mound of
earth. Only rough stone has been used, no mortar,
although legend has it that bullocks' blood was
used as an adhesive.

The Tuatha De Danann built many of these underground dwellings around Ireland, some of them large enough to have accommodated almost forty people, such numbers often composed of several families. Usually, there is one inconspicuous entrance but several exits affording speedy escape.

On manoeuvring the entrance to Brugh of the Boyne, one passes through a long low gallery which leads to a higher broader chamber. Substances found in many of these chambers in West Connaught are the accumulated debris of food used by man, along with ornaments of bronze, weapons, and primitive jewellery. In the walls of some of the chambers, hollowed out bunks appear, which could have served as beds or as graves.

The most famous of these underground caverns is Brugh of the Boyne, New Grange. Built by Eochard Ollathair, a celebrated King of the Tuatha De Danann, as a place of residence for himself and his family, the chamber also served as a place of burial for the chiefs of the tribe.

So a gracious and gifted race were subjected to the undoubted humiliation of hiding underground in order to survive. Who is to say that the small characters of Irish folklore (who also live underground) are not the descendants of this great race, the Tuatha De Danann?

the fairies in new ross

When moonlight
Near moonlight
Tips the rock and waving wood;
When moonlight
Near moonlight
Silvers o'er the sleeping flood;
When yew-tops
With dew-drops
Sparkle o'er deserted graves;
'Tis then we fly
Through the welkin high,
Then we sail o'er the yellow waves.
                    —*Anonymous*

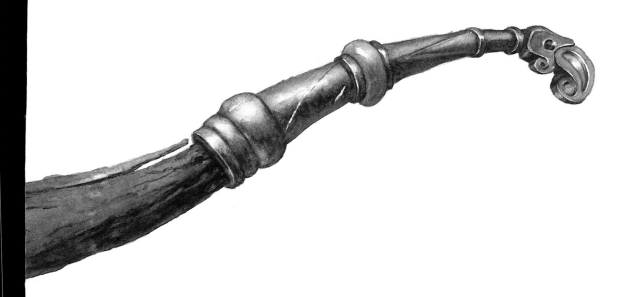

BIBLIOGRAPHY

The modern version of a Leprechaun's souterrain home is taken from *The Crock of Gold* by James Stephens (Macmillan, 1912).

Michael O'Sullivan and the Friendly Leprechaun is adapted from a Crofton Croker tale in *Fairy Legends of the South of Ireland*.

The following tales are adapted from tales in *Irish Folklore* by Rev. John O'Hanlon (Glasgow: Cameron and Ferguson): *Brave O'Kennedy and the Pooka*; *The Fir Darrig and the Black Pudding*; *O'Carroll's Banshee*; *Balor of the Evil Eye*.

The Kildare Pooka is adapted from a tale by Patrick Kennedy, published in *Great Folk Tales of Ireland* by Mary McGarry (Frederick Mueller Ltd, London).

Cold Iron Spurs and the Pooka is adapted from a tale recorded in Irish by Irish Folklore Commission (Ms. Vol. 157, 632–6).

Other bibliography consulted during research:

A Handbook of Irish Folklore, O'Sulleabhain (Singing Tree Press)

Ancient Legends, Mystic Charms and Superstitions of Ireland, Lady Wilde (Ward and Downey)

The Erotic World of Faery, Duffy (Panther Books)

Fairy and Folk Tales of Ireland, edited by W. B. Yeats (Colin Smythe)

Fairy Legends from Donegal (C.B.E. at University College, Dublin)

Fians, Fairies and Picts, Mae Ritchie (Keegan Paul)

Folk Literature of the British Isles, Norton (Scarecrow Press)

The Folktale, Stith Thompson (Dryden Press)

Highland and Fairy Legends, Macdougall (D. S. Brewer)

Legendary Fictions of the Irish Celts, Kennedy (Singing Tree Press)

Legends from Ireland, O'Sullivan (B. T. Batsford Ltd.)

Old Celtic Romances, P. W. Joyce (Gill and Macmillan)

Tales and Legends of Ireland, Monica Cosens (Harrap)

Ulster Folk Lore, Elizabeth Andrews (Eliot Stock)

West Irish Folk Tales and Romances, William Laramine (Irish University Press)

notes

bad cess to ye – bad luck to you

bohereen – lane

cairn – a pyramid of rough stones set up as a landmark or monument

cashel – castle

ceilidh – organised Irish country dancing and singing, often in a neighbour's house

delph – earthenware crockery

druid – a pre-Christian priest/wizard

dun – fort or fortified place

Early Mythological Cycle – a "Cycle" is a group of stories. This group of stories was related orally over hundreds of years before it was finally written down circa 400 A.D. The events they describe, however, are much older than this and are thought to date back to before the Bronze Age (2000 B.C.). The stories of the Early Mythological Cycle concern the adventures of the Tuatha De Danann.

fort – an underground dwelling, usually inhabited by fairies

frieze coat – heavy old-fashioned overcoat with pleats

frock coat – three-quarter length top coat

keening – bemoaning the death of a close friend or relative

Lough Derg – the lower of the Shannon Lakes

Maeve – Queen Maeve of Connaught, the western province of Ireland

megalith – stone-built monument of prehistoric age

Mourne Mountains – spectacular mountains in the north-eastern corner of Ireland

oxter – arm

pipes – oilleann pipes—a musical instrument native to Ireland, similar to bagpipes in tone and principal, but without a mouthpiece

pookawn goat – an old ugly male goat with long hooped horns

Sidhe – (pronounced *she*) tiny Irish fairies, far smaller than the Leprechaun and the Fir Darrig. The Sidhe live together in hosts. Their abode is usually an underground cavern, hollowed out and crowned on the surface by a hazel bush, fairy tree, or a ring of stones called a fairy fort.

spalpeen – term of abuse meaning rascal

squall – choppy storm

skelp – clout

Tuatha De Danann – in Irish mythology, the Tuatha De Danann were one of the first tribes to inhabit Ireland. They were tall, well-built, handsome and fair. It is thought they came from Greece via Scandinavia. They had magical powers and were mighty warriors, defeating the Firbolg in a famous battle, the First Battle of Moytura.

The Ulster Cycle – a collection of old stories dealing with the adventures of Cu Chulainn, the Hound of Ulster. These stories are set around the time of Christ, but were related orally for many hundreds of years before being set down in manuscripts after the fifth century A.D.

wake – a social gathering held in the house of the deceased, in order to honour the person's memory. Often developed into a lively party.

whet my whistle – to keep one's mouth from getting too dry

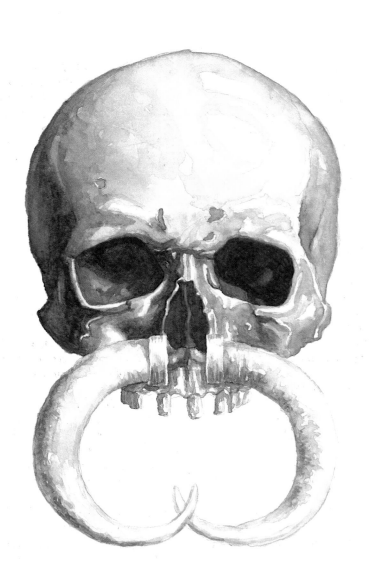